Palabras que debemos aprender antes de leer

anota

base

campeonato

jardines

liga

plato

www.rourkeeducationalmedia.com

Edición: Luana K. Mitten
Ilustración: Bob Reese
Composición y dirección de arte: Renee Brady
Traducción: Yanitzia Canetti
Adaptación, edición y producción de la versión en español de Cambridge BrickHouse, Inc.

Library of Congress Cataloging-in-Publication Data

Karapetkova, Holly
 ¿Está ulula en primera? / Holly Karapetkova.
    p. cm. -- (Little Birdie Books)
ISBN 978-1-61810-526-4 (soft cover - Spanish)
ISBN 978-1-63430-322-4 (hard cover - Spanish)
ISBN 978-1-62169-028-3 (e-Book - Spanish)
ISBN 978-1-61236-021-8 (soft cover - English)
ISBN 978-1-61741-817-4 (hard cover - English)
ISBN 978-1-61236-733-0 (e-Book - English)
Library of Congress Control Number: 2015944613

*Scan for Related Titles
and Teacher Resources*

Also Available as:

Rourke Educational Media
Printed in the United States of America,
North Mankato, Minnesota

rourkeeducationalmedia.com

customerservice@rourkeeducationalmedia.com • PO Box 643328 Vero Beach, Florida 32964

¿Está Ulula en primera?

Holly Karapetkova

ilustrado por Bob Reese

Hoy es el gran juego. Los Animales del Bosque juegan contra Los Animales del Pantano por el Campeonato de la Liga Menor.

La lechuza Ulula y el castor Casimiro juegan para Los Animales del Bosque. Ulula juega en primera base. Casimiro juega en los jardines. A ellos les encanta el béisbol.

Los Animales del Pantano parecen
buenos.

—¿Crees que podamos ganar, Ulula?
—pregunta la osa Melosa. Melosa es la
lanzadora de Los Animales del Bosque.

—No sé —dice Ulula—. Los Animales del Pantano son buenos, pero nosotros también.

Es hora de empezar el juego. Melosa lanza la primera bola. ¡Es una bola buena!

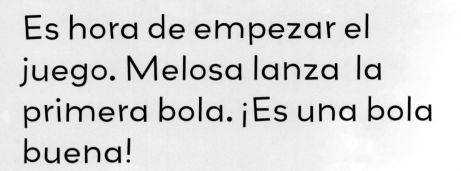

Al final del juego, Los Animales del Bosque y Los Animales del Pantano están empatados una a una. Ulula está al bate. ¡Pump! Batea la bola. ¡Ulula está en primera!

15

Ahora Casimiro está al bate. Batea la bola y corre a primera. ¡Ulula está en segunda!

Finalmente, le toca el turno a Melosa. Ella le da duro a la bola. Ulula corre a tercera base. Luego corre hasta el plato. ¡Ulula anota! Los Animales del Bosque ganan el campeonato.

—¡Felicidades! —dicen Los Animales del Pantano—. Ustedes son REALMENTE buenos.

—Al igual que ustedes, que jugaron muy bien —dice Ulula.

21

Actvidades después de la lectura

El cuento y tú...

¿Qué equipos están jugando béisbol?

¿Quién anota la carrera ganadora?

¿Cómo muestran los ganadores su buen espíritu deportivo al final del juego? ¿Cómo muestran los perdedores su buen espíritu deportivo?

Comenta cómo puedes demostrar tu buen espíritu deportivo en el patio de recreo de tu escuela.

Palabras que aprendiste...

Las siguienes palabras están relacionadas con el juego de béisbol pero también tienen otro significado. Elige tres palabras y escribe oraciones para ilustrar ambos significados.

anota	empatados	plato
base	jardines	primera
campeonato	Liga	segunda

Podrías... planear un juego en tu escuela.

- Decide qué juego vas a organizar.

- ¿Cuáles son las reglas para jugar este juego?

- ¿A quién invitarás para que juegue este juego contigo?

- Decide quién estará en cada equipo.

- ¿Cómo llevarás la puntuación de cada equipo?

Acerca de la autora

Holly Karapetkova vive en Arlington, Virginia, con su familia y sus dos perros. Le gusta ver a su hijo jugar béisbol, y le encanta escribir libros para niños.

Acerca del ilustrador

Bob Reese comenzó su carrera en el arte a los 17 años, trabajando para Walt Disney. Entre sus proyectos están la animación de las películas *Sleeping Beauty*, *The Sword and the Stone* y *Paul Bunyan*. Trabajó además para Bob Clampett y Hanna Barbera Studios. Reside en Utah y disfruta pasar tiempo con sus dos hijas, sus cinco nietos y un gato llamado Venus.

ER   Hood, Susan.

            Too-Tall Paul, too-
            small Paul.

$16.90

DATE			

A Note to Parents

Welcome to REAL KIDS READERS, a series of phonics-based books for children who are beginning to read. In the classroom, educators use phonics to teach children how to sound out unfamiliar words, providing a firm foundation for reading skills. At home, you can use REAL KIDS READERS to reinforce and build on that foundation, because the books follow the same basic phonic guidelines that children learn in school.

Of course the best way to help your child become a good reader is to make the experience fun—and REAL KIDS READERS do that, too. With their realistic story lines and lively characters, the books engage children's imaginations. With their clean design and sparkling photographs, they provide picture clues that help new readers decipher the text. The combination is sure to entertain young children and make them truly want to read.

REAL KIDS READERS have been developed at three distinct levels to make it easy for children to read at their own pace.

- LEVEL 1 is for children who are just beginning to read.
- LEVEL 2 is for children who can read with help.
- LEVEL 3 is for children who can read on their own.

A controlled vocabulary provides the framework at each level. Repetition, rhyme, and humor help increase word skills. Because children can understand the words and follow the stories, they quickly develop confidence. They go back to each book again and again, increasing their proficiency and sense of accomplishment, until they're ready to move on to the next level. The result is a rich and rewarding experience that will help them develop a lifelong love of reading.

For my Paul
—S. H.

Special thanks to Lands' End, Dodgeville, WI, for providing clothing
and to Hanna Andersson, Portland, OR, for providing Sue's dress.

Produced by DWAI / Seventeenth Street Productions, Inc.
Reading Specialist: Virginia Grant Clammer

Library of Congress Cataloging-in-Publication Data
Hood, Susan.
  Too-Tall Paul, Too-Small Paul / Susan Hood ; photographs by Dorothy Handelman.
        p.   cm. — (Real kids readers. Level 2)
  Summary: Two boys, one who thinks he is too tall and the other who feels too short,
become friends and teach their classmates not to judge them because of their size.
  ISBN 0-7613-2021-0 (lib. bdg.). — ISBN 0-7613-2046-6 (pbk.)
  [1. Size—Fiction. 2. Friendship—Fiction. 3. Stories in rhyme.] I. Handelman, Dorothy, ill.
II. Title. III. Series.
PZ8.3.H7577To   1998
[E]—dc21   98-10251
                                                                                 CIP
                                                                                 AC

pbk: 10 9 8 7 6 5 4 3 2 1
lib: 10 9 8 7 6 5 4 3 2 1

Too-Tall Paul, Too-Small Paul

By Susan Hood

Photographs by Dorothy Handelman

M

The Millbrook Press

Brookfield, Connecticut

My name is Paul, and I am tall.
At home this is not odd at all.
My dad is tall. My mom is, too.
So is my older sister, Sue.

5

But here at school I am so tall
that some kids call me Too-Tall Paul!

When I'm in line, I feel so dumb.
I stick out like a big sore thumb.

I do not fit well in my chair.
I hate it when kids point and stare.

In class there is another Paul,
and some kids call him Too-Small Paul.
He cannot reach his shelf or hooks.
He has to stand up on his books!

13

No one plays with Paul in gym.
No one throws the ball to him.

Kids don't pick him for their side.
He hangs his head and wants to hide.

It hurts us when they call us names
and when we cannot play their games.
The kids are smart, so they should know
you cannot choose how big you grow.

Shrimp Big foot

Most days I wish I were not tall.
I wish that I were small, like Paul.

So it is funny when I see
Paul wants to be as tall as me.

Sometimes it's good to be so tall.
It helps when I play basketball.

Sometimes it's good to be so small.
Paul twists and turns, while I just fall.

23

24

Now we're friends. I play with Paul.
I do not care that he is small.
Paul does not seem to care at all
that I am very, very tall.

We laugh a lot. We goof and grin.
We are good pals, so we both win.
I help Paul. He helps me, too.
There is not much we cannot do.

The most excellent book of how
to be a **magician**

Have you ever wanted to be a magician? This
book will tell you everything you need to know
to amaze your friends with spectacular tricks,
illusions. It is packed with your powers of
secret magician's tips, and hints for putting on a
perfect performance!

Other titles from Copper Beech Books:
The most excellent book of how to be a puppeteer
The most excellent book of how to be a card tricks

Peter Eldin The most excellent book of how to be a

The most
excellent book
of how to be a
magician
with easy step-by-step
instructions for a
brilliant perfo

We give a magic show one day.
The kids all clap. They yell, "Hooray!"

29

Now they don't call me Too-Tall Paul.
And no one says that Paul is small.
These days, in class and in the halls,
kids call us The Amazing Pauls!

31

Phonic Guidelines

Use the following guidelines to help your child read the words in *Too-Tall Paul, Too-Small Paul.*

Short Vowels

When two consonants surround a vowel, the sound of the vowel is usually short. This means you pronounce *a* as in apple, *e* as in egg, *i* as in igloo, *o* as in octopus, and *u* as in umbrella. Short-vowel words in this story include: *big, but, dad, fit, gym, has, him, his, kids, lot, mom, not, pals, win.*

Short-Vowel Words with Consonant Blends

When two or more different consonants are side by side, they usually blend to make a combined sound. In this story, short-vowel words with consonant blends include: *clap, class, grin, hangs, help, just, stick, twists.*

Double Consonants

When two identical consonants appear side by side, one of them is silent. In this story, double-consonants appear in the short-vowel words *odd, well, yell,* and in the *all-*family words *all, ball, call, halls, small, tall.*

R-Controlled Vowels

When a vowel is followed by the letter *r,* its sound is changed by the *r.* In this story, words with r-controlled vowels include: *are, for, hurts, smart, turns.*

Long Vowel and Silent E

If a word has a vowel and ends with an *e,* usually the vowel is long and the *e* is silent. Long vowels are pronounced the same way as their alphabet names. In this story, words with a long vowel and silent *e* include: *games, hate, hide, home, like, line, name, side.*

Double Vowels

When two vowels are side by side, usually the first vowel is long and the second vowel is silent. Double-vowel words in this story include: *days, feel, plays, reach, see, seem.*

Diphthongs

Sometimes when two vowels (or a vowel and a consonant) are side by side, they combine to make a diphthong—a sound that is different from long or short vowel sounds. Diphthongs are: *au/aw, ew, oi/oy, ou/ow.* In this story, words with diphthongs include: *how, now, Paul, point, out.*

Consonant Digraphs

Sometimes when two different consonants are side by side, they make a digraph that represents a single new sound. Consonant digraphs are: *ch, sh, th, wh.* In this story, words with digraphs include: *much, shelf, that, there, these, they, this, when, while, wish, with.*

Silent Consonants

Sometimes when two different consonants appear side by side, one of them is silent. In this story, words with silent consonants include: *dumb, know, pick, thumb.*

Sight Words

Sight words are those words that a reader must learn to recognize immediately—by sight—instead of by sounding them out. They occur with high frequency in easy texts. Sight words not included in the above categories are: *a, and, as, at, be, both, could, does, friends, give, here, I, in, is, most, my, no, on, one, or, says, school, should, sister, so, some, too, up, us, very, were, you.*